Bingo Explores the Farm

This book is dedicated to kids who explore their world and challenge their limits.

CPSIA Tracking Label Information: Printing by Coburn Printing Ink, Job Number 12-1206, Date of Production - June 2012, Printed in Hong Kong.

Library of Congress Cataloging-in-Publication Data available.

Hard Cover ISBN 13: 978-0-9839827-0-8
Soft Cover ISBN 13: 978-0-9839827-1-5

For additional information about Bingo visit www.bingoadventures.com.

The Bingo the Cat Series
Bingo's Big Adventure
Bingo Explores the Farm

Bingo Explores the Farm

by Julia King

KING PUBLISHING

I am a kitty explorer named Bingo, and I like to call myself a Mighty Adventurer. However, this morning I have not been able to find an adventure . . . yet.

I want to drive this car because it's just my size, but it seems to be broken. This old thing will not start no matter how long I sit here! What in the world is wrong with this hunk of junk?

Maybe I should check under the hood . . . or inspect the steering wheel.

I know! It's probably a broken gas pedal!

4

Oh dear, I am not a mechanic. I am only a cat. I do not have tools or even hands to use them. I must admit my adventure is not starting well.

Grrrrr! This car is so frustrating! Only what can I do about it? I think I need to get some help. Hey now! I see someone coming!

What good luck! My best friend Jimmy is here. He can help me. He is older and wiser than I am. He knows things that I do not.

As he approaches I ask him, "Jimmy, can you fix my car?"

The yellow fur between his eyes squishes together in concentration as he looks at my rusty car.

"Bingo, I don't think you will be driving *anywhere* today. Don't you know? We cats can't drive!" Jimmy explains.

"*But* . . . I will look at your car anyway. BACK OFF while I check under the hood!"

My word! Jimmy is a grouch. Sometimes he is not the best friend for me. Instead of fighting with him . . . I am leaving!

I am bored and I feel grumpy. I am disappointed that I have not found a new adventure.

Maybe I will wander with my four legs, look with my keen eyes, and sniff with my sensitive nose until I find a new adventure.

Hmmm . . .
          What is *that* ahead?

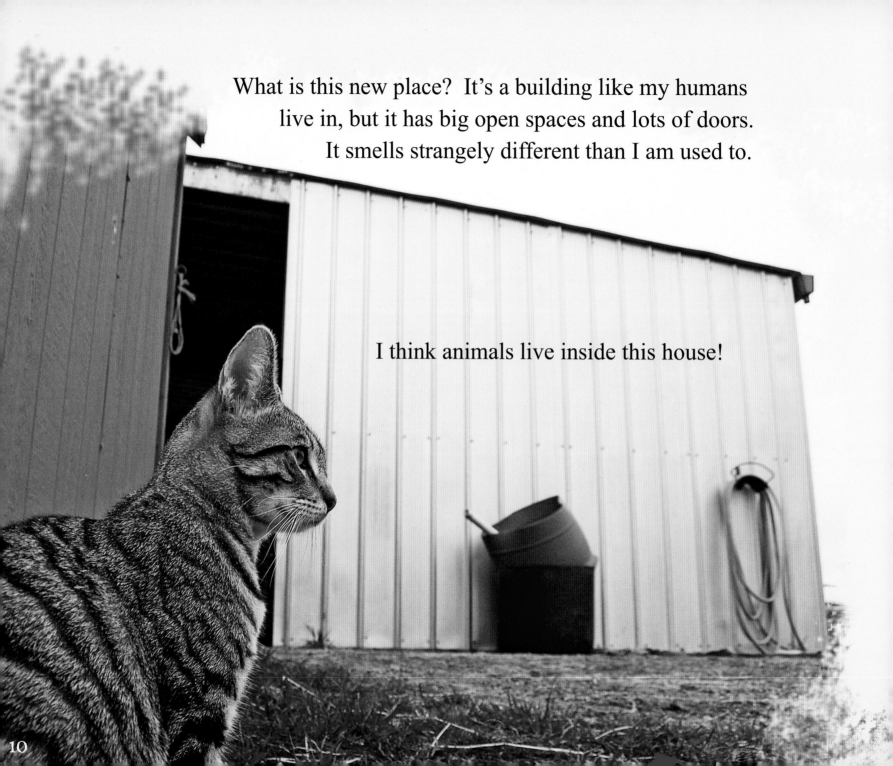

What is this new place? It's a building like my humans live in, but it has big open spaces and lots of doors. It smells strangely different than I am used to.

I think animals live inside this house!

Only . . . where are they?

11

Walking around the building, I see strange metal pipes. Spotted reflections dance on the rounded surfaces, but I have no idea why these tall bars are here.

I can't climb up the bars, but I can walk *under* them.

We cats slip through little spaces that other creatures cannot. We are sneaky that way.

I have found a gigantic bowl inside the building. It has a wheel, but it's different than my broken car.

I wonder what it's used for. The large wheel beneath it must roll the bowl around while it carries a lot of *something*.

My nose tells me that the something is. . .

STINKY!

Peeee-yew!

I should get out of here before I smell stinky too.

Long, dark shadows cover the floor, but because I'm a brave explorer, I'm not afraid. I am alert and I am using my cat senses to make sure the mysterious animals that live here don't surprise me.

I know there should be someone inside this empty building. What is this place and where is everyone?

Near the building I see gigantic bricks of dried grass. Are these grass bricks food for someone?

The grass bricks feel pokey to my paws, but I can still climb them. They smell nice because they have the scent of springtime inside them.

Somehow, I don't believe the humans can eat this stuff. But huge rodents might eat it. I would *like* to meet big mice. Mmmmmm. Big mice could be tasty!

I see no mice up here, so I am still curious . . . What animal eats this much grass?

I think the animals are outside! They are not in their house right now, just as I am not in mine.

I have been searching in the wrong place to meet the animals who live here.

Now I know what today's adventure is!
It is solving the mystery of who lives in this building!

My body is strong, so I can run and find them!

I see an animal out in the field with long, spindly legs and gigantic, round feet. It's definitely not a big mouse!
If I creep up slowly, maybe I can sniff this creature's nose.
I smell an adventure happening now!

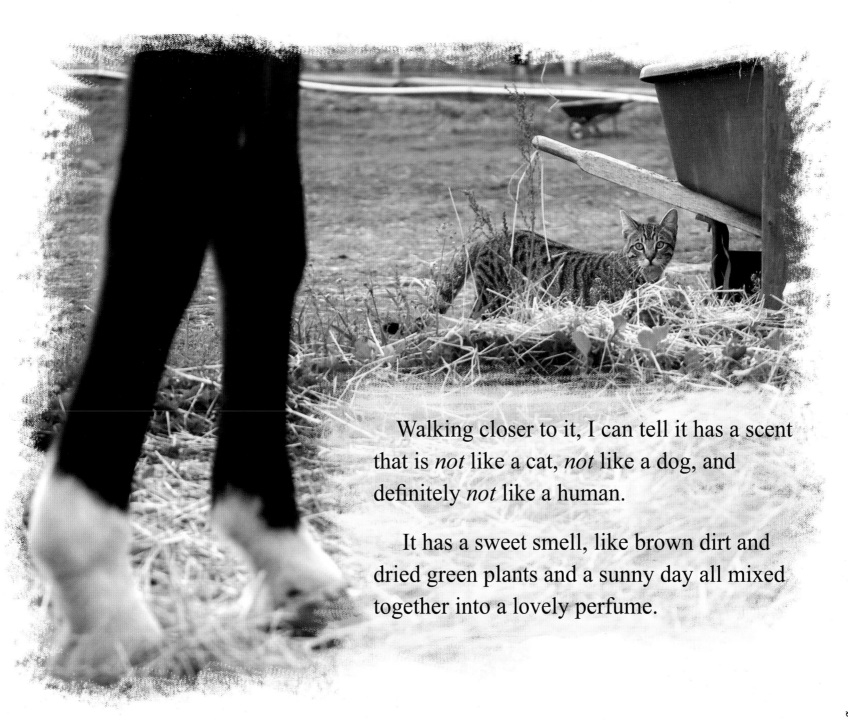

Walking closer to it, I can tell it has a scent that is *not* like a cat, *not* like a dog, and definitely *not* like a human.

It has a sweet smell, like brown dirt and dried green plants and a sunny day all mixed together into a lovely perfume.

This animal is looking at me!
It has dark, soft eyes that remind
me of nighttime.

Pieces of dried grass hang from this creature's mouth!

Aha! It is eating grass from the bricks in the building. Its huge mouth is full of grass and it is chewing quietly. But what if it were hungry for a cat?

Would it want to eat me for a snack?

That would be bad!

Naaaw . . . I don't think it wants to eat me!

This animal's head blocks the sky! I can't see around it, so I'm a wee bit nervous, even though I'm Bingo, the Mighty Adventurer. I may have to call myself "Bingo, the Tiny Adventurer" after meeting this animal.

But I *like* it! Do you see how long its whiskers are? It even has dirt in its nose!

"Hey you! Silly little fur ball! You're much too small to play with horses. You'd better get out of their pen," a loud voice exclaims.

I know that voice. It's the Tall Lady! *She is my human.* She brought me home to live on her farm.

"Bingo, horses can be frisky. You should find somewhere else to play," the Tall Lady warns me.

Did she say *horses*?
    So that's what these animals are called!

Wait a minute . . . What is this other horse doing?
This bright orange horse is leaping. It launches high into the air.
It is spectacular!
I don't think I can jump like that.

Is this horse acting frisky? *I think this is what the Tall Lady means!*
Horses are not *only* quiet, grass-eating creatures, they can be spunky too.

Should I play with
it or should I go?

I think it can jump
to the sky.
Can I?
I just don't know . . .

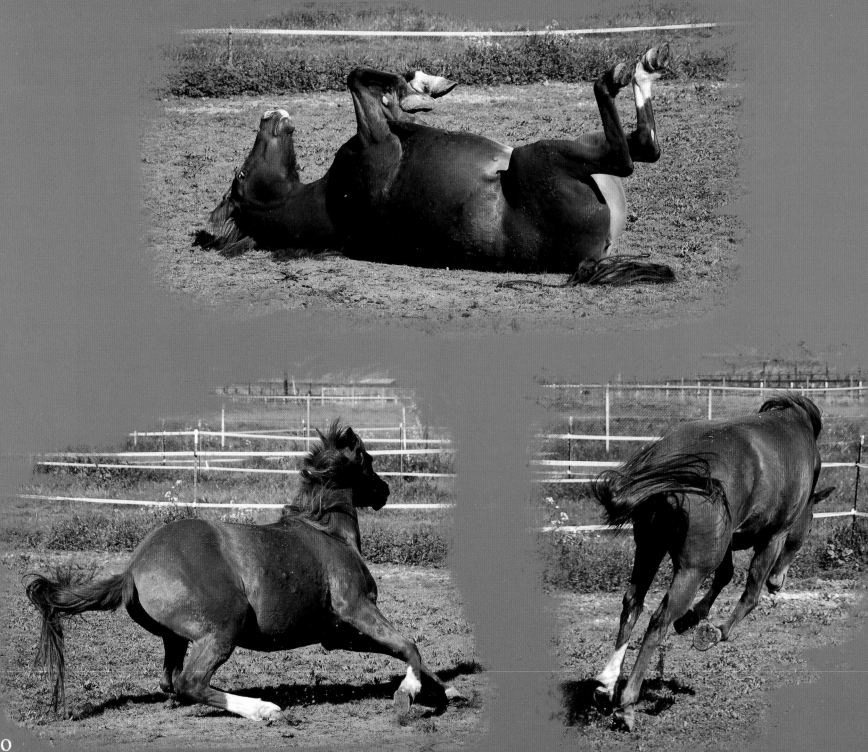

Ever since this horse started bucking and rolling, I have the wrong feeling in my bones . . . Watching it, I feel my fur fluff! It puffs! It tingles!

Why does my body feel strange? What is wrong with my fur? Why is my fur standing up? Does this mean I'm scared?

Maybe the
Tall Lady is right;
I should only watch
these horses from
the *outside* of
their pen.

Uh oh . . .
       time to go!

Oh . . . I am drooping with sadness because I have not discovered the *right* adventure. I am supposed to be a Mighty Adventurer, but I am having no luck.

"Binnnngooooo." From nearby I hear my name called. Then I hear a louder shout, "BINNG-GOOOO!"

Someone is calling me!

I see the boy named Wyatt who lives with me and the Tall Lady. Sometimes, he chases me like a wild thing. But even though he bothers me, I still like him.

Why is he calling me? Since I am a cat, I am always curious. I will go see him.

Wyatt is dragging a stick for me!
How did he know I'd like to chase a twig?
It wiggles and rattles against the sand
like a lizard's tail, and I must inspect it.
I am a cat, so I cannot resist . . .
I have been looking for this
kind of adventure!

I didn't know he
could play with me
like this.

Now Wyatt wants to pet me. I am glad he can be a gentle friend too. It makes my throat rumble with a soft purr.

A boy is not like a car with wheels and strange pedals. Cats can't drive cars anyway. A boy is not like a top-cat who pushes me around. I want to be my own boss. And a boy is not like a horse who makes me feel as tiny as an ant.

A boy!
        A boy is just right.

I think discovering these different feelings has been my adventure today.

And just maybe my adventure was to find the right someone to play with, and I think this boy is purr-fect.

The End

Questions Beyond Bingo Explores the Farm

1. What are the rows of plants growing behind Bingo and his old rusty car? How do you know?

   The vegetable crop in the story is corn. Tall green corn stocks and their silky-tasseled ears can be seen in the background behind Bingo's car.

2. What is the name of the building that Bingo finds on the farm?

   The barn. The horses on Bingo's farm live in the barn when it rains because their fields become too wet and slippery to play in. Barns protect animals from bad weather.

3. What is the name of the large bowl with a wheel beneath it, and what does it carry?

   It's a wheelbarrow and it carries horse manure.

4. What are the brownish-green bricks of dried grass called? Hay bales!

5. What are the tall metal pipes called? What do they do?

   The metal pipes within the story are called pipe panels and they are used as fencing for horses or other farm animals.

6. Did you notice the sandy area where Bingo and the boy play? Do you know what it is called and what it is used for?

   It is called a riding arena. It is where the horses are exercised and ridden.

7. Which of the five senses does Bingo use when he describes his adventure on the farm? Give an example of how he uses these senses.

   For example: Sight. Bingo sees Jimmy the cat coming.

8. How does Bingo know that he is scared? How do you know when you are scared? How do you feel or listen to your body when you are afraid?

9. How do you think Bingo feels after he discovers the boy can play with him?

10. Choose your favorite farm animal. Can you imagine what the animal feels or thinks, and write a short story about life from his or her point of view?

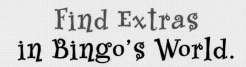

Did You Know?

These are backgrounds from inside the book.
(flip back to find and inspect these textures in the story.)

Did you know this is tin?
Tin is a thin metal used for the roof and outside walls on a barn.

Did you know this is sun-bleached wood?
This wood is from the horse barn. It is used for walls.

Did you know this is horse hair?
Horses have short dense fur to protect them from bad weather.

Did you know this is paint from Bingo's metal car?
It is rusty in some spots from age.

Did you know this is peeling paint?
Paint flakes fall off wood after years of being in the sun and rain.

Find Extras in Bingo's World.

Can you find the four cloud horses?
They were made from real photos of horses playing.

Can you find these bird boxes?
Birds use them yearly for nesting and raising chicks.

Can you find the bluebird?
Bluebirds nest every year in the boxes around Bingo's farm.

Can you find the soaring bird?
Vultures are often seen high in the sky around Bingo's farm.

Can you find the red wheelbarrow?
This is a kid-sized wheelbarrow that the boy plays with.

The Cast

BINGO
AS
"THE MIGHTY ADVENTURER"

JIMMY
AS
"THE TOP CAT"

SHARPIE
AS
"THE FRISKY HORSE"

WYATT
AS
"THE BOY"

GEMMA
AS
"THE LONG-FACED HORSE"

NOW WHO'S READY FOR A NAP?!?!

KING PUBLISHING

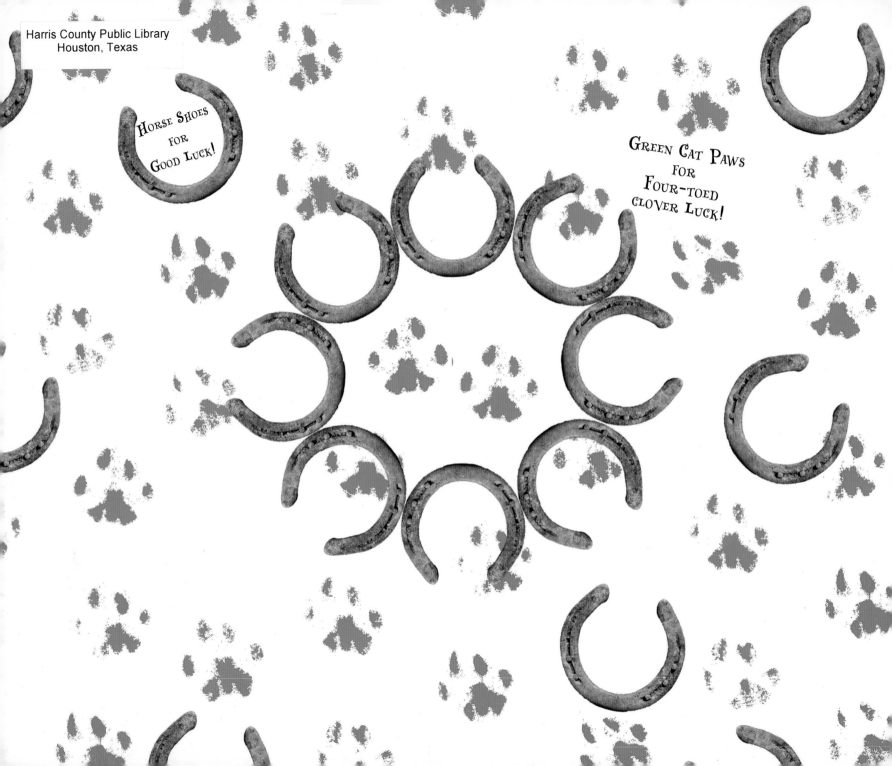

Horse Shoes
for
Good Luck!

Green Cat Paws
for
Four-toed
Clover Luck!